Praise for *The Imagination Station®* books

I really liked [*Captured on the High Seas*] because the adventure is a fun way to learn about history. It taught me to be brave and to put others first.
> —Melina, age 7, Elkhart, Indiana

I love that the books are easy to read. I want to keep reading because the books are full of adventure!
> —Kanaan, age 8, Midlothian, Texas

I love how the book showed people sharing and putting others before themselves. This book made learning about history fun.
> —Abbie, age 9, El Paso, Texas

This [second book in the] exciting saga . . . [has] gold nuggets of God's word essential for training and equipping [kids]. Nancy Sanders does a wonderful job crafting a world you'll feel like you're a part of.
> —Scott M., homeschool dad and radio talk-show host
> St. Johns, Michigan

More praise for *The Imagination Station®* books

I can't think of a better way for children to learn about United States history.

—Sharon B., public school teacher, Munster, Indiana

This is a great book because it has lots of action and adventure. I like that the characters never give up.

—Sophia, age 9, Colorado Springs, Colorado

Another powerful story that takes today's reader back in time on a realistic hair-raising adventure. I couldn't put it down.

—Mona P., reading tutor, Appleton, Maine

I was very thankful to have a book to read to our daughters that was exciting enough to hold their attention and still uphold and encourage the values that we are trying to teach them.

—Tiffany K., mom, Eureka, Illinois

FOCUS ON THE FAMILY PRESENTS

Captured on the High Seas

BOOK 14

MARIANNE HERING • NANCY I. SANDERS
CREATIVE DIRECTION BY PAUL MCCUSKER
ILLUSTRATED BY DAVID HOHN

TYNDALE

FOCUS ON THE FAMILY • ADVENTURES IN ODYSSEY®
TYNDALE HOUSE PUBLISHERS, INC. • CAROL STREAM, ILLINOIS

Captured on the High Seas
© 2014 Focus on the Family

ISBN: 978-1-58997-775-4

A Focus on the Family book published by Tyndale House Publishers, Inc., Carol Stream, Illinois 60188.

Focus on the Family and Adventures in Odyssey, and the accompanying logos and designs, are federally registered trademarks, and The Imagination Station is a federally registered trademark of Focus on the Family, 8605 Explorer Drive, Colorado Springs, CO 80920.

TYNDALE and Tyndale's quill logo are registered trademarks of Tyndale House Publishers, Inc.

Cover design by Michael Heath | Magnus Creative

For Library of Congress Cataloging-in-Publication Data for this title, visit http://www.loc.gov/help/contact-general.html.

Printed in the United States of America

1 2 3 4 5 6 7 8 9 / 19 18 17 16 15 14

For manufacturing information regarding this product, please call 1-800-323-9400.

To Amanda,

Your example of godliness, your cheerful smile, and your life of sharing the Good News with kids are an inspiration to us all. (Plus, I can't wait to see what you crochet next!)

—NIS

Contents

Prologue

Mr. Whittaker is a friendly but mysterious inventor. He lives and works at Whit's End. It's an old house with lots of rooms. One of those rooms is his workshop.

Mr. Whittaker's favorite invention is the Imagination Station. It's kind of like a time machine. Cousins Patrick and Beth like the invention too.

Patrick and Beth have gone on many exciting adventures in it. They have visited a Viking village. They have stayed with the Pilgrims at Plymouth. And they have even met a cannibal king in Fiji.

One day Patrick and Beth raced into the soda shop at Whit's End. They told Whit they were leaving on a family trip. They were planning to visit places and museums from the American Revolution.

Mr. Whittaker thought Patrick and Beth would like to meet Paul Revere. So the cousins went on an Imagination Station trip to Massachusetts.

In Concord they saw the start of the Revolutionary War. Then Patrick and Beth climbed into the Imagination Station to leave. Moments later a musket ball hit the window of the time machine. The musket ball left a big crack.

Patrick and Beth didn't return to Whit's End. Instead, they landed on a large ship.

What happened?

Had they landed on the ship because the Imagination Station was broken?

Or had Whit sent them there on purpose?

Most important, would they ever make it back to Whit's End?

Captain's Orders

Beth felt as if she were in a giant rocking chair. She couldn't stop moving back and forth. A spray of icy water splashed on her face. She was confused.

Beth looked around for Patrick. The Imagination Station hadn't returned them to Whit's End as usual.

Patrick spoke from where he was sitting beside Beth. He pointed above them and said, "That's an American flag from the

Revolutionary War."

Beth blinked her eyes and tried to see in the darkness. The moon was shining. It cast a faint glow of silver light. *Where are we?* she wondered.

She and Patrick had just been in Concord. They had warned the American colonists that the British were coming. Now she was on the deck of a sailing ship. Tall masts towered over her.

She saw dark figures moving around above. Sailors were probably working the sails.

Everything was quiet. It was creepy.

Beth now studied the flag high above them. On the front was a snake against a yellow background. Across the bottom were the words "Don't Tread on Me."

Beth realized she was holding Patrick's

hand. She let go and stood up. "Why didn't we go back to Whit's End?" she asked.

She thought about the answer to her own question.

The windshield cracked, Beth thought. *Maybe the Imagination Station had been damaged.*

Patrick stood up beside her. "We must have landed somewhere in the middle of the war," he said.

"Then why is it so quiet?" Beth asked. She could see a little bit better in the darkness now. Her eyes were adjusting to the moonlight. She saw a tall shadow move in the darkness behind Patrick. The figure put something against Patrick's back.

"Who goes there?" a low voice asked.

There was the dull sound of metal clicking. "Don't shoot!" Patrick said. He raised both hands in the air.

Beth stepped toward the shadow. It was a young man with a pistol.

"We're here to help," Beth said in a kind voice.

A look of surprise flashed across the young man's face.

"A girl?" he asked.

Beth stepped closer. She could see the young man more clearly now. A black hat with a wide brim sat on his head. He wore a striped shirt and a handkerchief around his neck.

Beth guessed that he was one of the sailors. He looked about fifteen years old.

The young man lowered the pistol. "What are you doing here?" he asked quietly.

"I wish I knew the answer," Patrick said, arms still high in the air.

"This is no time to jest," the teen said. "All hands are supposed to be below deck. Those standing watch are allowed on deck. And sailors hoisting the sails may climb aloft." He glanced around as if making sure no one had seen them. "Get below. Now."

Patrick lowered his hands.

Beth wasn't sure which direction to go. She didn't move.

The sailor jerked his head toward the right. Beth hurried in that direction.

Patrick followed her.

The sailor came close behind.

The ship rocked back and forth. Beth reached out to grab the mast to steady herself. She saw a square hole in the floor. A ladder led into the darkness below.

Beth looked down at her clothes. She was still wearing the red dress from their last adventure.

Beth gathered her long skirts and turned around. She climbed backward down the ladder to the deck below.

Beth saw more sailors in the shadowy darkness. And cannons, too.

The sailor led them down another ladder to the next deck. He pulled aside a curtain. Then he pointed to a cramped space with a small bunk. "Next time be sure to obey the captain," he said.

"We didn't hear the captain give his orders," Beth said.

"The captain said no talking," the sailor said. "No lanterns. And no moving around below decks."

"But why?" Beth asked.

"What's going on?" Patrick asked.

The sailor's eyebrows arched upward. "Why don't you know?" he asked. "We're sneaking past a British warship. We'll be blasted to pieces if the enemy hears us."

The sailor turned to leave. He looked back over his shoulder. "Stay here," he said. "I'll be back when my watch is over."

And then he was gone.

Sail Ho!

Patrick sat down on the bunk. He scooted back until he pressed against the ship's wall. That left room for Beth to sit down. Then he reached over and pulled the curtain closed. His head bumped the ceiling as he sat back again.

Patrick kept his voice low. "Did the Imagination Station break? Or did Mr. Whittaker send us here on purpose?"

"Our clothes are the same as before," she

whispered. "Usually we get new ones. Maybe we landed here by accident."

Patrick looked down at his clothes. He was still wearing a blue coat with a double row of buttons. His tan pants stopped just below his knees. He had tall stockings and leather shoes with brass buckles. He reached up and felt for his triangle hat. It was still there.

Then he noticed something. "I don't have my cane anymore," he said quietly.

Beth held up something in her hand. "I found this in my pocket," she said.

A tangy smell stung Patrick's nose. It was an onion.

"Check your pockets," Beth said.

Patrick reached into his pants pockets. Empty. Then he reached inside the large front pockets of his jacket. He touched something with his right hand. He pulled out a lumpy leather pouch.

Patrick reached inside the bag. "It's full of smooth, round stones," he said. "They feel like marbles."

Now he felt excited. "Whit gave us new gifts to use," Patrick said. "He must have planned for us to come here."

Beth smiled and nodded. Then she put a finger to her lips. "Shhh," she whispered.

Patrick settled back in the bunk. He wondered, *What is this adventure going to be?*

Patrick listened to the creaking of the ship. He pressed against the wooden wall to keep from sliding around. The boat was really rocking now.

Shouts erupted from up on deck. "Huzza! Huzza!" Then suddenly the curtain was pulled back with a *whoosh.*

A dim light glowed. Behind the light was the sailor. He was holding a lantern.

"It's safe now," the young man said. "We've sailed past the British warship."

The sailor lowered the lantern. "My name is James," he said.

Patrick saluted. "And I'm Patrick."

Beth smiled at James. "I'm Beth."

"Let's go up on deck," James said. "We'll get some fresh air."

Patrick waited for Beth to climb out. Then he hopped off the bunk.

The cousins followed James. He led them up two sets of ladders to the top deck. A pink glow filled the sky to the east. The sun was rising over the water. More sailors were busy with ropes and sails.

James blew out the lantern and hung it on a hook.

Patrick felt the strong wind tug at his hat. He held on to it with his hand. He grabbed the ship's railing with his other hand. The ship heaved up and then down again. Patrick's stomach moved with it.

It was hard to keep his balance. He saw that Beth was having a hard time too.

James grinned at them. "This is my second time at sea," he said. "It takes a little while to get your sea legs."

James looked at Patrick and then at Beth. "This is our first day out," he said, "and I don't know the new crew yet. It's a bit unusual to have a girl on board. They're not allowed on the ship. Not even if they're family. How did you get here?"

"It's hard to explain," Beth said.

Patrick had an idea. "I don't think *how* we got here is important," he said. "It's more important *why* we're here. We've come to help win the war against the British."

James studied them a minute. Then he nodded. "That's why I enlisted on the

Royal Louis. I help carry gunpowder to the cannons during the battles. I'm a powder monkey."

Just then a loud shout came from high above them. "Sail ho!" a man cried.

James turned and stared out over the ship's railing. He pointed toward the rising sun. "It's another British warship!" he cried. "And she's coming our way!"

Cannons Roar

Beth looked out over the crashing waves.
She couldn't see anything at first. Then the
Royal Louis crested a tall wave.

"There it is!" she shouted into the wind.
She could see a ship in the far distance.

A whistle sounded. "All hands ahoy!"
came the cry.

Sailors rushed up on deck from below.
They climbed up ropes to reach the sails
high above them.

Beth watched as more sails were let down. They spread open like white wings.

A wave washed over the front of the *Royal Louis*. Cold water swirled around Beth's feet. The water got the hem of her dress wet.

James called out to them. "The captain's trying to outrun the warship," he said. "I've got to get below."

"What can we do to help?" Beth asked.

"Follow me!" James said.

Beth turned to look at Patrick behind her. His face looked pale. He held on to the side of the ship.

"Are you okay?" she asked.

He nodded. "Let's go," he said.

Beth and Patrick followed James down the first ladder. A row of cannons lined both sides of this deck. A group of teenage boys had gathered there.

Beth saw that about half of the boys were white. Half were black like James. Most were about the same age as James. But one boy with red hair looked younger. Beth guessed he was about her age.

James called out to the group. "Lash everything here and below," he said. "It will be hard work sailing in this wind."

The boys tied down everything that could slip or slide.

Patrick showed Beth how to tie knots in the ropes. His hands shook. He dropped the rope a few times.

Beth knew he wasn't feeling well. But he still managed to work hard.

Each wave jerked them up

and then down again. Icy water splashed
through the ceiling and onto their faces.
Beth tasted the salty drops. Her dress was
completely soaked now. Her fingers were
stiff and cold. She was shivering. And she
was hungry.

Another whistle sounded from above
them. "Prepare to fire!" came the cry.

Sailors rushed down the ladder to get
the cannons ready. One sailor called out,
"Powder monkeys to the ready!"

Beth and Patrick hurried after James and
the other teens. They climbed down another
ladder. And then another. They came to a
deck that was almost totally dark.

Beth covered her nose. What was that
horrible smell down here? It smelled like
a mix of dirty bathroom, rotten eggs, and
moldy, wet leaves.

Poor Patrick! He looked as if he might gag. "Maybe you should go back up to the cannons," she said to him.

Patrick shook his head.

They both helped carry small loads of gunpowder to the upper deck. Then they headed down below again. Beth and Patrick tried to keep up with James and the others.

"Fire!" a voice cried.

Kaboom! Kaboom! Cannons roared. Smoke poured down through the ladder holes. It stung her eyes and nose.

Just then Beth heard another blast from the other ship.

KABOOM!

Beth heard the sound of breaking wood. The *Royal Louis* jerked beneath her feet. She fell to the deck.

They'd been hit!

Surrender

Patrick grabbed one of the gunpowder barrels to steady himself. He saw James reach out a hand to Beth. The teen pulled Beth to her feet.

"That was just a warning shot," James said.

"It felt like more than a warning," Beth said.

"I don't think we had too much damage," James said. He stood still as if he was listening.

Patrick heard the sound of the whistle

coming from above.

A low murmur ran through the group. The other boys hurried back up the ladder. Only Patrick and Beth stayed below deck with James.

Patrick heard hurried footsteps and men shouting on the upper decks.

"What's going on?" Patrick asked.

"The captain knows we're no match for a British warship. He signaled our surrender," James said. He clenched his fists. "The British will take us as prisoners of war. I'll have to give over my pistol."

Patrick sat down on an empty barrel. He still felt ill. But he knew they had a problem.

"Our clothes," he said.

"What about them?" Beth asked.

"I'm not dressed like the other sailors," Patrick said. "And you're still in a dress. It's not safe for a girl."

"It's not safe for any of us," James said with a deep frown. "They'll send me to the West Indies as a slave."

"They're allowed to do that?" Beth asked.

"We're their prisoners," James said. "They can do whatever they want."

Patrick looked up at James. "We need to blend in. Do you have any extra clothes we could change into?"

"Yes, but we must hurry," James said. He moved away. Then he stopped and looked back at Beth. "You should cut your hair," he said.

"What? I'm not cutting my hair," Beth said.

"You need to look like a boy," James said. "It'll be safer."

"Do you have a cap?" she asked. "I can tuck my hair inside to look like a boy."

James nodded. "Stay here," he said. "I'll get you both some clothes."

James was back in a minute with a canvas bag. It had dry clothes and jackets inside. He dropped it at Beth's feet. "Everything you need is in here," he said. "I'm going to get other supplies while you change." He quickly climbed the ladder and was out of sight.

Beth disappeared behind a stack of barrels to change clothes.

Patrick waited for her. He used the time to silently ask God for help. *Keep Beth safe,* he prayed and then added, *Keep all of us safe. And don't let them make James a slave.*

Beth came out wearing sailor's clothes and a jacket. She had a soft gray cap on her head. "I hope this works," she said. She clicked the heels of her brown boots. She tucked her hair inside the cap.

Patrick was relieved that she looked a little more like a young boy now.

Patrick grabbed some clothes. Then he went behind the barrels to change. The dry clothes felt warm.

James came down the ladder. A large canvas bag was draped over his shoulder. He held a large pewter mug with one hand. In the other hand was a stack of biscuits. Steam rose from the mug.

"Hot coffee," James said. "And hardtack."

"Is that another name for biscuits?" Beth asked.

James nodded and then showed them how to eat it. He dipped the hardtack into the coffee. Then he nibbled on the biscuit.

He handed the mug to Patrick. Patrick drank the hot coffee. The warmth spread through him. Eating bits of hardtack made his stomach feel better. Patrick handed Beth the mug.

Beth sipped the coffee and frowned. "Ewww," she said.

A face appeared at the hole in the deck above them.

"All prisoners topside," the man said in a British accent. "On th' double."

James motioned for the cousins to follow him. He moved toward the ladder with his sea bag.

Beth put down the mug and followed James up the ladder.

Patrick was the last one up. They gathered on the top deck with all the other sailors. The British sailors were there too. They held guns, clubs, and pistols. The Americans were unarmed.

One of the British sailors barked a command. He ordered all the Americans to gather into groups. Then they were ordered over to one side of the ship. Rowboats waited for them in the water below.

Patrick, Beth, and James climbed down a rope ladder into a rowboat. The soldiers rowed through the wind and icy waves. All the passengers were soaked to the skin. No one had the energy or the will to speak.

The waves were huge. Patrick felt as if they were riding a bucking horse. He started to feel queasy again. And cold.

He turned back to look at the *Royal Louis*. It was already sailing away with its new British crew.

Patrick shivered. He and Beth were in the hands of the enemy. He wondered, *What was going to happen to them now?*

Troublemaker

Patrick stood on the deck of the British
warship. He was lined up with the other
American prisoners. Beth and James stood
on either side of him. He felt better in the
fresh air. But he was still worried.

A tall man stood on a raised deck. He
wore a fancy blue jacket with gold trim. His
three-cornered hat matched his jacket. His
pants and vest were white with gold buttons.
He gripped a book in his hands.

The British crew stood along the ship's railing. The men held their weapons at the ready.

"Attention!" the tall man shouted to them. "I am Captain Bazely. You are prisoners of war on His Majesty's ship, the *Amphion*. Officers and crew will be taken below and held under guard. Cabin boys and powder monkeys will be under my command. You will be assigned duties to repair and clean the ship."

Captain Bazely opened his book. "March below deck if your name is called," he said. Then he called out a list of names. One by one the sailors were led away.

The captain read another list of names. Then more. Each time a different group of sailors was led away. Patrick watched the other powder monkeys go below deck. He heard a British crewman shouting at them to start repairs on the ship.

Everyone had been taken away. James, Patrick, and Beth were the only Americans left.

Captain Bazely looked down at his book and then up again. "Which one of you is James Forten?" he asked.

"I am, sir," James said. He stepped forward.

Captain Bazely said, "Your captain told me about you. He said you're the only powder monkey who knows his letters. You have received an education then?"

Patrick saw James square his shoulders. "Yes, sir," James said.

"Quite so. It will be your duty to teach my twelve-year-old son, Henry," the captain said. "He needs to learn to read and write." He turned to a nearby sailor who had a sunburned face. "Bring Henry to me."

The sailor saluted and then left the deck.

Captain Bazely looked in his book. "I have no more names on the ship's muster." He looked down at Patrick and Beth. "Are you cabin boys?"

Patrick and Beth looked at each other. Patrick didn't know what to say. Beth turned red but kept silent.

The captain pointed at Beth. "Your name, boy. What is it?"

Beth shoved her hands in her jacket pocket. She stared back at him. "My name is . . . Seth," she said.

"Quite so," the captain said. "You will help the cook."

One of the British sailors stepped up and led Beth away.

Patrick watched her go. It worried him

when they were separated. He hoped she could take care of herself.

"And your name, boy?" the captain asked.

"Patrick," Patrick said.

Just then the sunburned sailor returned. A wiry boy with messy hair followed him. He was dressed in a formal jacket. It had a double row of brass buttons. A handkerchief was tied around his neck.

Patrick noticed the boy's suit was dirty. He looked as if he needed a long, hot bath.

"Ah, Henry," Captain Bazely said. He turned to James. "Your orders, James, are to stay with Henry at all times. Small boys are nothing but trouble on a big warship like this. They can fall overboard, climb the rigging, or disarm the cannons."

"You want me to be a nanny, sir?" James asked.

"Yes," the captain said. "For Henry and for this child as well."

Patrick realized the captain meant *him*. He felt embarrassed. "I'm not a child," he said.

"I'll be the judge of what you are," the captain said. He turned on his heel and left.

Henry looked at Patrick and James. He grinned. "We'll have a jolly good time together!" He jumped up. Then he climbed on the lower ropes of the rigging.

"Get down from there," James said.

Henry ignored him. "Sailing is boring. So I tie knots in the ropes. And I stuff nuts in the cannons. I even taught the cook's parrot to steal coins. He snatches them with his beak and gives them to me. Now *that* was fun!"

James reached for the boy. "Henry—"

Henry pulled himself up to the next

rope. "The parrot was on a pirate's ship we captured," he said. "You should have seen the sword fights! And the cannon blasts! We blew that pirate ship to smithereens!"

Henry climbed up the rigging.

"Come down here!" James shouted.

Henry laughed. Up and up he climbed.

"Come on," James said to Patrick. "We've got to get him."

Patrick grabbed the lower ropes of the rigging.

James followed. "This boy is trouble," he said, grumbling.

Patrick wondered if Mr. Whittaker had really planned this. Had he put Patrick on a Revolutionary War ship to *babysit*?

Onion Jim

Beth followed the sunburned sailor below. British sailors hurried back and forth. This deck was wide open. But it was as crowded as a shopping mall during a sale.

Barrels were lashed to beams so they wouldn't roll.

Beth saw two rows of cannons. They were lined up against the sides of the deck. Their large iron bodies were tied down with ropes. The cannons creaked as the ship rocked up and down.

A large man with greasy red hair stood nearby. Beth could only see his back. He was busy cooking at a tall black stove. Beth held out her frozen hands toward the stove. She rubbed them together to warm them up.

"Ahoy, Cookie," the sailor said. "Seth's your new helper."

Cookie turned his big frame around. He wore a filthy apron over his sailor's clothes. He flipped a coin in the air, caught it, and put it in his pocket.

"This one is a bit skinny to be toting buckets," Cookie said.

The sailor nodded, turned around, and left.

Cookie looked at Beth and scowled. He looked closer at her.

Does he think I'm a girl? Beth wondered.

She was worried. Then she remembered the onion in her pocket. She pulled it out and held it up to distract him.

"Can you use this?" Beth asked the cook.

"I don't need an onion," Cookie said. "I've got barrels of them."

Beth saw that Cookie was missing a front tooth. "Oh no!" he said suddenly. "Onion Jim goes daft when he sees onions."

"Onion Jim?" Beth asked.

"Yes," said Cookie. "Onions are poison to birds. But he thinks they're sweet as treats. He ate one once and almost died. Put it away, now!"

A flurry of feathered wings burst into the cooking area. The flurry was screeching and squawking.

"Aaah!" Beth cried in surprise.

A parrot landed on her shoulder. "Give us the onion," the parrot squawked. "Pretty please."

"Too late," Cookie said. "Now Onion Jim knows you have an onion. He won't stop pestering you until you give it to him."

Cookie reached out a beefy hand. "Give it to me," he said. "I'll put it in my stew. That way he'll know you don't have it anymore. You can get another one from the hold."

Beth handed over the onion. Cookie grabbed it and then turned around. He started chopping the onion with a big knife.

"Give us the onion," Onion Jim squawked again. He poked his beak in Beth's pocket. He was looking for another onion. But the pocket was now empty.

Onion Jim snatched Beth's cap off her head. Then he dropped it on the floor.

Beth's hair fell to her shoulders. She panicked. She bent down, grabbed the cap, and stuffed her hair back underneath. Onion Jim flew to a nearby barrel.

Cookie turned around with bits of onion in his hand.

Beth's heart pounded hard. The cook hadn't seen a thing.

Cookie put the chopped onion in a pot of boiling stew. Then he set a piece of hardtack on the barrel. Onion Jim cocked his head. He looked at the biscuit sitting next to him.

The bird pecked at the hardtack with his beak. "Thank you, dearie," Onion Jim squawked. The bird sounded just like an old lady.

Beth giggled.

"Here," Cookie said. He handed Beth a pewter mug. Then he pushed a plate of beans toward her. He dropped a hard biscuit on top. "Take this down to the officer in the hold. Then come back double-quick. I need you to tote buckets of salt meat up here."

Onion Jim flew over and landed on Beth's shoulder. She reached up with one hand to hold on to her cap. She tried to shrug the bird off her shoulder. But Onion Jim wouldn't move. His claws clamped onto Beth.

Beth hurried down two sets of ladders into the hold. It smelled like an outhouse. The stink was so foul that she could hardly breathe.

A small lantern hung on a hook. The dim light shone on fat rats. They scurried away from Beth. She recognized barrels of gunpowder stacked in rows. There were different barrels, too. Beth guessed they were full of food and supplies.

Off to the side sat a man inside a metal cage. He wore an American officer's uniform.

"This is for you," Beth said. She pushed the plate and mug between the iron bars.

The prisoner took the plate and mug. "Thank you," he said. He sat down on his bunk. He placed the mug beside him.

"Hungry?" Beth asked.

The man looked up at her. "I'm Lieutenant Prescott in the Continental navy," he said. "They captured my ship a week ago."

"We got captured this morning," Beth said.

"You're American then," Lieutenant Prescott said. He took the biscuit and banged it on the floor. White flakes fell off. The flakes began to squirm and crawl.

"Eww," Beth said, stepping back.

"Weevils," the lieutenant said. "They get in the flour."

Onion Jim flew off Beth's shoulder and landed on a barrel. "Shiver me timbers!" he squawked. Onion Jim flapped his wings. Then he flew up the ladder to the deck above.

The lieutenant chomped into the hard biscuit.

Beth felt sorry for him. She moved closer to the cage and said softly, "Is there anything I can do to help?" she asked.

Lieutenant Prescott looked at the ladder and then back at Beth.

"You could fetch my sword," he whispered. He pointed toward the barrels of gunpowder. "They stowed my sea chest behind the barrels." He slipped a small key through the bars. "The sword is hidden in a secret compartment on the bottom." He told her how to find the sword.

Beth went behind the barrels and found the chest. She used the key to open the trunk. She followed Lieutenant Prescott's instructions. She pulled out different pieces of clothing and a canvas bag. Beth found the false bottom, opened it, and lifted out his sword.

Beth looked up through the square hole. No one was coming down the ladder.

Beth crept from behind the barrels. She handed the sword to the lieutenant. He hid it under a pile of straw. Beth raced back to the trunk and locked it up again.

Beth looked at the different barrels in the hold. An idea came to her. She passed a barrel full of onions and grabbed one. She hid the onion in her jacket pocket. Then she gave Lieutenant Prescott his key.

"Thank you," the lieutenant said.

"The cook might come looking for me," she said. "I have to go back." She took the empty plate and mug from the lieutenant. Then she hurried back up the ladder.

She wanted to find Patrick. He could help with her idea. It would keep the *Amphion* from capturing more American ships.

If the plan worked.

A Game of Marbles

Patrick looked up. Henry was in the rigging, twenty feet above him.

The boat pitched forward. Patrick's jacket blew open. His heavy leather pouch fell out. It dropped straight as an arrow to the deck below.

"What was that?" James asked.

"Marbles," Patrick said. Then he had an idea. He shouted at the boy, "Henry! We challenge you to a game of marbles!"

Henry paused from his climbing and looked down. "Nobody has any marbles on board," he shouted.

"I do!" Patrick shouted back.

Henry began to climb down.

Patrick and James dropped to the deck. Henry soon followed. Patrick grabbed his leather pouch.

"Let's play," Henry said. "We'll have a jolly good time together."

James held up his hand. "Not so fast," he said. "First you have to practice your letters. And then we'll play marbles."

Henry shrugged. "Let's go to Father's cabin," he said. "There are quills and parchment in there."

Henry led them below deck. His father's cabin was at the back of the ship.

Inside the cabin was a bunk, a sea chest, and a small desk. Patrick spotted an hourglass and compass on the desk. There were also quills, ink, and paper.

James made sure Henry copied all of his letters. Patrick noticed that they wrote in cursive. James's lettering looked beautiful with its curls and slant.

"Now copy this sentence for the letter *A*," James said to Henry. "In Adam's Fall we sinned all."

James watched Henry practice a few lines. Then he announced it was time to stop. Patrick pulled the bag of marbles out of his pocket. The three of them crouched on the floor.

Henry took a piece of chalk out of his pocket. Then he drew a circle on the floor. Patrick put the smaller marbles in the middle of the circle.

Patrick took the first turn. He aimed the big shooter marble at the other marbles. He hit one of the marbles in the middle. But he missed the second shot. The ship's rocking made it difficult to aim.

Next, it was Henry's turn. "I can do better than that," he said. Henry shot and hit two marbles. Then he missed.

Now it was James's turn.

James crouched down even lower to the floor. He took careful aim. He hit his marble. Then the next. One by one James hit all the rest out of the circle.

Patrick whistled. "You're good," he said to James.

"That happened by chance," Henry said.

James grinned. "Do you think so?"

"You can't do that again," Henry said.

"Let's give him another try," Patrick said.

They set up the game and gave James the shooter.

He didn't miss a single shot.

Patrick was impressed. It looked as if Henry was too.

James played another game with the same results. Captain Bazely walked in as they finished.

"Nobody shoots a perfect game!" Henry cried, jumping to his feet. "Father, watch what James can do!"

Captain Bazely watched as James displayed his skill. The captain said, "You are a skilled lad." Then he turned toward the desk. He picked up the paper Henry had been writing on. "But I'm more impressed with the letters." The captain looked at James. "Did you teach Henry to write this?"

James stood up. "Yes, sir!" he said. "I'll see to it, sir, that Henry practices his reading, too. I'll teach him from a Bible in my bag."

The captain nodded. "Quite so. Be sure to teach Patrick how to read as well." He turned and headed outside.

"I know how to read and write," Patrick told James.

"You can help me with Henry's lessons, then," James said. "Let's get my Bible."

They left the captain's cabin. Patrick saw Beth's head peek out of a hole in the deck. He was glad to see she was okay.

"There you are," Beth said. She climbed up the ladder to stand before the boys. She straightened her jacket. "Can you help me carry salt meat up from the hold?" she asked Patrick.

Patrick looked at James.

"Go ahead," James said. "You can help with the reading lessons later."

"Reading lessons!" Henry cried. "I've had enough schooling for one day." Henry ran off.

James groaned and raced after him.

"Listen," Beth said when she was alone with Patrick. "The cook needs someone to carry small casks of meat up from the hold. We can fill our casks with gunpowder between trips. Then we'll dump the powder over the side of the ship. We can empty out the barrels of gunpowder. There won't be any left to fire the cannons."

Patrick thought a minute. That sounded as if it would take too much time. And it would be dangerous. "What if we get caught?" he asked.

"Do you have a better idea?" Beth asked. "We should do *something* to help the American ships."

Patrick didn't know what else to do. Mr. Whittaker couldn't have put him on the ship to play marbles.

Beth tugged at Patrick's arm. "Let's get started," she said. "Danger or no danger, we have to try to help."

Sword Fight

Patrick helped Beth for the next couple of days. They brought casks of salt meat up from the hold. Then they moved the casks to the kitchen.

They dumped the salt meat into a large water barrel. The meat soaked so the salt would come out of the meat.

Patrick and Beth stayed in the hold between trips. They took gunpowder from large barrels and filled different casks. They moved the empty gunpowder barrels to the back of the hold. Then they dragged the full ones forward.

Patrick would check that no British crew members were looking. Then Beth would dump the powder out through the gun ports.

"Cannons are useless without gunpowder," Lieutenant Prescott said to encourage them. "This British ship won't capture any more prisoners for a while."

Patrick liked the feeling of danger. He liked sneaking around the ship. He liked knowing he was helping his country.

One morning Patrick was filling up his cask with gunpowder. Beth was nearby filling hers. Lieutenant Prescott slept in his cage nearby.

Patrick looked out over all the gunpowder barrels they'd emptied. They still had five more to go.

Patrick tipped one of the full barrels on its side. He began to carefully roll it forward. But right at that moment the ship dipped. The barrel rolled loose and banged into a wall.

Patrick looked up. He saw a British sailor coming down the ladder.

Patrick motioned to Beth to hide.

Beth ducked behind a stack of sea chests. Patrick hid behind a group of barrels.

The sailor reached the bottom of the ladder. He looked inside the cage. "I've been hearing noises down here," he said to Lieutenant Prescott. "You don't have any friends trying to help you escape, do you?"

Lieutenant Prescott stood and stretched slowly. "Let me see," he said. He kicked at the straw and looked under his bunk. "No one here, unless you count the rats."

"Very funny," the British sailor said. "I know I heard something." He turned and peered into the dark shadows.

Patrick held his breath. He crouched down as low as possible.

The sailor's footsteps came closer to Patrick. "The noise sounded like moving barrels," the sailor said. "And why is that gunpowder barrel open?"

Patrick could hear the sailor's breath. The British man was closing in on him!

Dear God, Patrick prayed silently. *Please don't let us be caught!*

Just then Patrick heard a loud crash. He peeked between the barrels.

Lieutenant Prescott had kicked down the door to his cage. The bars were ripped right out of the wood.

The lieutenant had his sword in hand. He slashed it through the air.

"I don't need help to escape from you British dogs!" he said. "Come and fight me!"

The sailor jumped back and drew his sword.

Clash!

Clang!

Swords struck together as the men fought.

The lieutenant was clearly the better swordsman. He lured the British sailor *away* from Patrick.

Crash! Food barrels fell over as the men jumped between them.

Patrick heard running feet on the deck above. British sailors clattered down the ladder.

"What's going on?" one sailor shouted.

"An escaped American," another cried.

Soon the hold was filled with British crew members. Even Cookie was there.

Shouts and noise and confusion were everywhere.

Patrick crawled to Beth's hiding spot. "Let's pretend we ran down to watch too," he said. "Now, while they're all watching the fight."

The sailors waved their pistols and swords. They cheered for their countryman.

"Huzza! Huzza!" Cookie cried.

"Cut him to the quick," the others said.

Nobody noticed as the cousins joined the group watching the fight.

Just then Captain Bazely hurried down the ladder. He aimed his pistol at the two men fighting. He shouted, "Put down your arms!"

The men stopped fighting. They dropped their swords. Both were breathing hard.

"Explain yourselves," Captain Bazely said.

The British sailor spoke up. "Lieutenant Prescott escaped and attacked me with his sword," he said. "He should be flogged and shot!"

Patrick felt terrible. He knew Lieutenant Prescott had done this to save them.

Captain Bazely narrowed his eyes. "No," he said. "American officers are too valuable. We can trade them for British prisoners."

Captain Bazely pointed his pistol at

Lieutenant Prescott. "Back inside the cage," he said. He shouted to an officer nearby, "Fix that door. Make certain he can't escape again. I want two guards to watch him day and night."

The officer saluted. "Aye, Captain," he said.

The captain turned to go. His eye caught Patrick and Beth. He frowned. "What are you boys doing here?" he asked. "What's in your casks?"

Patrick's stomach dropped down to his feet. He didn't know what to say. The captain might not shoot an American officer. But he and Beth were just cabin boys.

Just then Cookie stepped out from the crowd. "They're bringing up salt meat," Cookie said. "I sent them down here."

The captain nodded. "Quite so. Carry on."

Patrick's hands shook as he carried his

cask up the ladder. Beth followed behind him.

Patrick waited until they were alone on deck. Then he whispered to Beth, "Now what will we do? We can't empty the rest of the barrels now. Not with two guards nearby."

Just then James and Henry came toward them. James was lecturing Henry angrily. Henry looked at the deck with a frown.

"What's wrong?" Patrick asked.

"Henry sneaked away from me during the commotion," James said. "I found him on the gun deck throwing the rammers overboard!"

"What are rammers?" Beth asked.

Henry looked at Beth as if she had asked a stupid question.

"They're long sticks," James said. Sailors

use them to pack the powder in the cannons."

"I remember them," Beth said. "From the battle when we were captured."

"What will your father say?" James said to Henry. "Without the rammers the cannons are useless. Do you think he'll be pleased with you? Do you want to be captured?"

Patrick and Beth looked at each other. They had the same idea.

Henry laughed. "Wouldn't that be a jolly good time?" he said. "I'd like to be a prisoner. I wouldn't have to practice my letters or learn to read."

"Don't talk like a fool," James said. "From now on you'll be like *my* captive. I'm not letting you out of my sight. Come on, we have lessons to attend to."

Henry whined as he followed James

across the deck.

Patrick waited until nobody was looking. Then he and Beth went over to the gun ports. They dumped the gunpowder out of their casks.

"Let's meet later after I serve the captain his meal," Beth said. "We have to figure out how to finish the job Henry started."

Patrick nodded. But he was worried. Dumping the gunpowder over the side of the ship seemed easy. Destroying the rammers was another thing entirely. It was likely they'd be caught.

Unwelcome News

Beth pushed open the door to the captain's cabin. Captain Bazely was busy at his desk. He was writing on a sheet of parchment.

Beth set a plate of food on a small table. The captain ignored her.

She walked back to the kitchen area. Cookie stood next to the stove. Onion Jim was perched on his shoulder.

The cook tossed a gold coin up in the air. Onion Jim tried to catch it. But the cook

was quicker and grabbed it. Then he held
the prize up for Beth to see.

"Pirate's gold from the ship we captured,"
he said. "Onion Jim wasn't the only prize we
took from the pirates."

Cookie stuffed the gold coin in his apron
pocket. "The captain will want his tea," he
said. He pointed to a pot hanging on a hook
near the stove.

Onion Jim screeched. "Give us a ride,"
he squawked. He flew to Beth's shoulder.
She tried to shoo him away. But the bird
clung to her jacket. Beth slipped out of the
garment, and the bird flew off.

"Not now," Beth said to him. She hung
her jacket up on a nearby hook. She picked
up the hot pot of tea with a rag. Then she
headed to the captain's cabin.

Beth passed a row of cannons as she left

the kitchen deck. She noted the long sticks next to each one. Several sailors busied themselves scrubbing the deck. *I wish no one else was here,* she thought. *I'd pitch those rammers into the sea right now.*

She saw British sailors in the hold. They were busy guarding several American prisoners who had moved there. She couldn't get close to Lieutenant Prescott.

Beth carried the tea into the captain's cabin. He now sat at a small table. He was eating the food she'd brought him earlier.

She set the tea next to him. A sailor walked in behind her. "You called, Captain?" he asked.

"Yes," Captain Bazely said. "It's time to drop off the rebel prisoners at the *Old Jersey.*"

Beth poured tea into a pewter mug.

Captain Bazely said. "Orders are to sail north to New York at once."

Beth's hands shook as she finished pouring the tea. She hurried back to Cookie and filled the pot with fresh water. She put the pot back on the hook next to the stove. She wanted to tell Patrick the news right away.

Onion Jim hopped up and down on one of the barrels. "Give us a ride, dearie," he squawked like an old lady. "Pretty please?"

Cookie looked up from the stove. He was stirring a big pot. He frowned.

"That bird won't be quiet until you give him a ride," Cookie said. "Take him along while you bring food to the crew." He pointed to a bucket on the floor. "There's some potatoes to deliver. Then come right back."

Beth groaned.

Onion Jim flapped his wings and landed on Beth's shoulder. He pecked at her cap. But she held on to it tightly with one hand.

Beth took the food to the crew members. She served the potatoes and then hurried off to look for Patrick. "You better behave yourself," she said to Onion Jim.

She found Patrick on the top deck. He was sitting on a coil of rope. James and Henry sat next to him. Each of them was sewing a piece of white cloth.

Without looking up, Patrick said, "James is teaching Henry to make a ditty bag. I'm learning too."

"What's a ditty bag?" Beth asked.

Patrick finished a stitch. He cut a piece of thread with a small knife. Then he held up the bag.

"Sailors use them to hold their personal

stuff," he said. "Like a comb or lump of soap."

Beth felt the sun warm her skin, but her mood was cool. Beth turned her bucket upside down to make a stool. She sat on it and looked around. She wanted to make sure no one could hear her.

Patrick noticed her serious expression. "What's wrong, Beth?" he asked.

Onion Jim squawked, "What's wrong, Beth?" The bird sounded just like Patrick.

"Seth," Patrick said quickly. "I meant Seth."

Beth pressed her lips together in a thin line. "Captain Bazely just gave orders to sail to New York. He's going to put us on the prison ship there."

Patrick, Henry, and James all stopped their work.

Beth saw a look of fear flash across

James's face.

"What does this mean?" Patrick asked.

Henry shrugged. "We put all the prisoners on docked ships," he said. "Then we try to capture more."

"Those ships are floating graveyards," James said. "I've heard that most of the prisoners die."

Henry looked down at the ditty bag he was sewing. He shook his head. "They don't *all* die on the ships," he said. "A lot of them are sent to the West Indies to be slaves."

Beth gasped and looked at Patrick and James. "What are we going to do?" she asked.

The Declaration

Hearing the news about the slave trade stunned Patrick. He couldn't sew on the ditty bag any longer. He put down the fabric and the knife.

Beth looked shocked.

James said, "I was hoping it wouldn't be so soon."

Everyone sat without moving. *What can we do?* Patrick wondered. There was no answer to his question.

Henry looked up at them. He seemed puzzled. Then he seemed to understand what would happen. His mouth fell open. "Oh," he said. "Sorry."

"I have to get back to the kitchen," Beth said. She stood and picked up the empty bucket. She mumbled a cheerless good-bye and walked away.

Patrick heard Onion Jim squawk, "What's wrong, Beth?" as she climbed down the ladder.

A cold breeze passed over Patrick. The sunshine seemed to fade. He shivered.

James looked sad. "My grandfather was a slave. He told us terrible stories," he said. "My parents and I are free."

Patrick didn't know what to say.

"That's why I joined up to fight," James said. "I heard the very first reading of the

Declaration of Independence. It was read aloud to the colonists on July 8, 1776. I stood in front of the statehouse with them."

"That was Philadelphia, right?" Patrick said.

"Philadelphia is my home," James said. He stood up and held on to the rail. He looked out over the wide blue sea. "We hold these truths to be self-evident, that all men are created equal," he said slowly and softly.

Patrick knew he was quoting from the Declaration of Independence.

James continued, "That they are endowed by their Creator with certain unalienable rights, that among these are life, liberty, and the pursuit of happiness."

Patrick felt his heart stir at the words. But he also felt angry. James could still be sold as a slave under American law. Blacks were still not free.

Patrick glanced at Henry. Henry kept his head down. He appeared to be hard at work on the ditty bag.

James leaned back against the rail. "I heard the very last sentence of the declaration too," he said. "That's when I decided to fight for liberty."

"What does that line say?" Patrick asked.

"And for the support of this Declaration," James said, "with a firm reliance on the protection of divine Providence, we mutually pledge to each other our lives, our fortunes, and our sacred honor."

Patrick had never heard that part before.

"That's why black soldiers are joining the fight," James said. "Both slave and free. Last month I saw George Washington. He and his troops marched through Philadelphia. The

members of the Rhode Island Regiment are black like I am. Blacks are fighting for the day when *everyone* will be free."

Patrick gaped at James. "You *saw* George Washington? In *person*?"

James nodded.

"I wish *I* could see him," Patrick said. "He's a hero."

James smiled. "Yes, he is."

Just then one of the British sailors approached them. "Are you James Forten?" he asked James.

"Yes, sir," James said.

"Captain Bazely wants to see you," the sailor said. "Come with me."

James turned to Patrick. "Look after Henry," he said. Then James and the sailor left quickly.

Patrick crouched down next to Henry.

"What do you think, Henry?" he asked carefully. "Do you want James to be sold as a slave?"

Henry shook his head. "No," he said.

"What can we do?" Patrick asked.

Henry was silent for a moment. Then he looked up at Patrick. "I will tell my father that we must protect James."

Patrick felt a twinge of hope. Did Henry have enough sway with his father? "Will he listen to you?"

"I'll make him listen," Henry said.

The boy leaped to his feet and bolted away.

Patrick ran after him.

An Offer of Safety

Beth carried the bucket back to the kitchen. The warmth of the stove surrounded her as she approached Cookie. He was stirring a pot of rice with a large spoon.

Onion Jim flew off her shoulder. He landed on the peg holding her jacket.

"The captain wants more tea," Cookie said. He put down the spoon.

Beth carried the pot to the captain's cabin. She stopped to pray outside the door.

She asked God to help James and the other prisoners.

Beth knocked on the door and entered the cabin. The captain was sitting at his desk. A leather book was open on his desk. He drummed his fingers on the desktop. *Tap. Tap. Tap.* He stared into space. He didn't seem to notice Beth at all.

Beth poured more tea into the pewter mug.

Just then a sailor appeared at the door. "James Forten, Captain," the sailor said. He motioned for James to enter the cabin. James stepped in. The sailor gave a slight salute and then left.

Beth took her time gathering up the dishes. She lifted the dirty plate off the little table. Then she reached for the silverware. She wanted to hear why the captain wanted to see James.

James took a few steps toward the captain. He stood with his hands folded in front of him. He glanced at Beth. He looked worried.

"James," Captain Bazely said. "You are aware that you are a prisoner."

"Yes, sir," James said.

"You are completely in my power," the captain said. "I can sell you to the West Indies. You are aware of that?"

"Yes, sir," James said.

Captain Bazely gazed at James for a moment. "Henry is a difficult boy," he said. "He isn't a bad child. He simply needs guidance. I believe you can give him that guidance, James."

"If you say so, sir," James said.

The captain's tone made Beth feel hopeful.

Captain Bazely said, "I want you to be Henry's companion. You will live in England as a free citizen. You will become part of our family. You will enjoy all the rights my family members would have. You need never be afraid of becoming a slave again."

Beth held her breath. This seemed too good to be true.

James took a deep breath and squared his shoulders. He stood straight and tall.

"Thank you, sir," James said, "but I must say no."

The captain looked up. He seemed startled.

Beth flinched. *No?*

James said, "Sir, I stand here a prisoner for my country. I will never, *never*, become a traitor."

Beth's heart flooded with emotion at

hearing these words. James was willing to die for America. He was giving up his own safety to fight for freedom.

The door flew open. Beth was surprised to see Henry rush through. Henry cried, "You can't sell James as a slave!"

Patrick arrived at the door. He was red-faced and breathless.

James stood still like a statue.

Beth looked at the captain. He wore a solemn expression. His eyes showed little emotion. "The choice isn't mine," he said to his son. "James has decided for himself."

A sailor appeared at the door. "The prison ship is in sight," he announced. "And a slave ship is also in the harbor. The first mate of the slave ship has boarded. He now requests permission to speak with you."

"Quite so," Captain Bazely said through

clenched teeth. "Permission granted."

The sailor left.

The captain looked at James. "I have offered you a chance for freedom," the captain said. "I hope the rebels appreciate your sacrifice."

A tall, gruff-looking man came to the captain's cabin. His black beard and moustache were full and thick. His jacket was tan-and-white striped. Beth thought it looked made of cotton. His hat had a wide brim.

The slave trader saluted the captain. Then he looked at James with a greedy smile. "I see you have at least one prisoner I can buy," the slave trader said.

All eyes were on the captain.

Captain Bazely glared at the tall man. Then he looked at James.

Beth was filled with worry. She bit her bottom lip and wondered, *What's going to happen now?*

Missing Coin

The captain's lips were pressed into a straight line.

"He is a fine lad," Captain Bazely said. "Strong. Smart. Educated. He'll bring in a fine profit."

James didn't move or flinch. Beth wondered what he was thinking.

The slave trader gave a wide but mean smile. "I'll be taking him now," he said.

Henry stared wide-eyed at his father. He

blinked back tears. "Father?" he said in a small voice.

The captain reached over and ruffled his son's hair. Then he looked at the slave trader.

"James is not meant for slavery," Captain Bazely said. "I've grown fond of him. So has my son. You'll have to take your pick from the other black prisoners. Not this one."

The slave trader looked surprised and then angry. "As you say," he said curtly. He turned in a huff and stomped out the door.

Beth breathed a sigh of relief. Patrick nodded at her.

Henry flung himself into his father's arms.

Captain Bazely hugged Henry and then sat down at his desk. He picked up a sheet of paper and his quill.

"James," he said, "I will write a letter to

the captain of the *Old Jersey*. This letter will note your fine character and courage. I'll ask him to put you on the list of exchanges. That may improve your chance of survival. But I cannot promise anything beyond that."

The captain paused. He looked James straight in the eyes. Then he said, "You're sure you—"

"I am honored that you would ask," James said, bowing. "But I cannot go to England."

"Gather your things, then," the captain said.

James turned to Patrick and Beth. The three of them walked out the door. Henry followed.

"That was a brave thing you did," Patrick said to Henry.

Henry shook his head. "I'm not happy," he said. "I want James to stay with me."

James patted him on the shoulder. "Thank you, Henry. But God is taking me elsewhere."

Beth left the boys to get her jacket from the kitchen. She also wanted to say good-bye to Onion Jim and Cookie.

The husky cook was busy chopping onions. He scowled when he saw Beth. He reached a beefy hand into the pocket of his apron. He pulled out a gold coin.

"My gold coin went missing," Cookie said. "I looked everywhere for it." His face turned red with anger. "And where did I find it?"

Beth was puzzled.

Cookie held the coin under Beth's nose. "In your jacket pocket! *My* gold!" he shouted. "You stole my gold!"

"I didn't steal it!" Beth said.

Onion Jim flew over to Beth with a loud

squawk. His wings flapped as he landed on Beth's shoulder. "What's wrong, Beth?" he asked. The bird sounded like Patrick.

"Beth?" Cookie said. "Hey, what's going on?"

Cookie swung his hand at the bird.

"Go away, bird!" Cookie said. "I'm going to give this thief a good thrashing!"

Onion Jim jumped around Beth's shoulder. His wings flapped, and his feet clawed at her. One of his talons hooked on Beth's cap and pulled it off. Beth's hair fell around her shoulders.

Onion Jim flew up and away.

Beth gasped. She scrambled to grab the wool hat from the floor.

"You're a girl!" Cookie shouted. "So you're a girl *and* a thief!"

Cookie grabbed Beth's arm.

Beth tried to pull away. Cookie tightened his grip.

"Guard!" Cookie shouted toward the ladder opening. "I need a guard!"

"All the soldiers are on deck. They're guarding the prisoners," Beth said. She tried to wriggle free. But Cookie held on to her with a firm grip. She stomped on his foot.

"Ouch!" Cookie cried.

Cookie grabbed some rope from the deck. Then he pushed Beth down into a nearby chair. He pinned her to the chair with one arm. He wrapped the rope around her with his other hand.

Beth kicked Cookie's leg.

"Hold still, you little rascal," Cookie said with a grunt.

Beth tried to push him away, but the cook was too strong. The rope pinched

Beth's arms and legs. Cookie tied her firmly to the chair.

Beth was trapped.

● ● ●

Henry followed Patrick and James. They joined the crowd of prisoners on the top deck. Hundreds of men waited to be taken to the prison ship.

Patrick scanned the faces around him. *Where is Beth?* he wondered.

Patrick heard a loud squawk and beating wings. Onion Jim landed on Patrick's shoulder. "You're a girl! Liar! Thief!" the parrot squawked.

"What?" Patrick asked.

The bird flew off and landed on a nearby rope.

Beth is in trouble, Patrick thought. He turned to James. "I have to find my cousin," he said and then rushed away.

He headed down a ladder to the gun deck below. Henry followed close behind. Patrick found Beth tied to the chair by the cook's stove. She looked at him wide-eyed and pressed her lips together.

The cook's back was toward Patrick. Cookie held an onion in one hand. A hot skillet was in the other hand. He looked ready to strike Beth with the skillet. He shouted at her, "There will be no prison ship for you, lassie. That's too good a punishment for a thief *and* a liar."

Henry whispered in Patrick's ear. "Watch this!" he said. "We'll have a jolly good time."

Patrick didn't have time to speak. Henry bolted over to one side of the deck. He ran to the row of cannons along the wall. Patrick didn't know what Henry planned to do. He

crouched behind a barrel near Beth's chair.

Patrick watched Henry pick up a rammer. The boy pushed it out the gun port.

Splash! Patrick heard it hit the water below.

Cookie spun around just as Henry pushed a second rammer overboard. "What's going on?" the cook cried. "What are you doing, boy?"

Cookie looked over at Beth and then back at Henry.

Henry pushed another rammer overboard. *Splash!*

"You rascal!" Cookie cried. "Belay there! Stop!"

"You can't tell me what to do," Henry said. "I'm the captain's son!"

"I don't care whose son you are! We need those rammers!" Cookie shouted. He took a few steps and then lunged toward Henry.

But Henry was too quick. He ran away with another rammer. At the closest gun port, he threw it overboard. Then he grabbed another.

Cookie was always too late to stop the boy. He shouted and waved the skillet in the air.

Patrick reached into his pocket. He found the knife James had given him for the ditty bag. Patrick sawed through one rope.

"Hurry!" Beth whispered.

Henry danced and dodged out of Cookie's way.

Patrick cut through the second rope. The ropes soon fell free.

Beth grabbed her cap from the deck.

"Come on!" Patrick whispered.

Patrick and Beth ran to the ladder. She stuffed her hair under the cap.

"No, you don't!" Cookie shouted. He turned from Henry and charged at her. The cook waved the skillet wildly in one hand. He was still holding the onion in his other hand.

Patrick pushed Beth toward the ladder. He knew the cook would catch them before they got very far.

Suddenly Onion Jim flew at Cookie. "Give us the onion," he squawked. "Pretty please."

Henry threw a rammer in front of Cookie. The cook tripped, dropped the skillet, and crashed to the floor.

13

The Prison Ship

Beth and Patrick raced up to the top deck.

"Patrick! Seth! Over here!" James called. "It's time to go!" He was standing near the rail.

Patrick and Beth pushed their way through the crowd of sailors. They finally arrived where James was.

James climbed down the rope ladder first. The ladder was about fifteen rungs long. He dropped into the small boat waiting underneath the ladder. The boat already held at least twenty men.

Patrick backed down the ladder next.

When he was at the tenth rung, Beth started down.

Patrick dropped into the boat. And then he looked up.

Cookie's red face appeared over the rail. The cook shook his fist and shouted at Beth, "You liar! You thief!" He reached over the side and grabbed the rope ladder. He gave it a mighty tug.

The sudden jerk threw Beth off balance. One of her feet slipped off the rope rung. Her leg got tangled in the rope. Suddenly she was dangling upside down from the ladder. She held her cap on with one hand.

Patrick gasped.

"Watch out!" James shouted. He pushed

past Patrick and grabbed Beth under the arms. "Untangle your legs."

Beth began to kick at the ladder. The motion pushed the boat away from the ship.

James's arms were stretched to their full length.

Patrick's heart beat wildly. "Seth is stuck!" he shouted to James. "Hold tight."

A British soldier said, "Hurry up, or we'll leave him hanging there. The birds will peck his eyes out."

Cookie bellowed with laughter. "Thief," he cried. "I hope you drown!" He tugged on the rope again.

The soldier looked at Cookie. "Why the shouting?" he called. "He's going to rot in prison. Isn't that enough?"

"Ow!" Beth cried. "It's my ankle!" Then she gave a sudden twist. Her foot came free. She

and James fell to the bottom of the boat.

"Your boot," Patrick said. "It's still in the rope!"

The soldier leaned over with an oar. He knocked the boot out of the ropes.

Splash! It landed in the water. Patrick fished it out. He turned the boot over. Water gushed out.

Beth and James climbed onto the boat's wide bench.

Beth stared down at her sock. "At least I don't have holes in my socks," she said. She looked at James. "Thanks," she said. "That was scary."

James smiled. "At your service," he said.

Patrick handed the boot to Beth.

She slipped it back on. "Yuck. It's cold and squishy," she said.

The soldier plunged the oar into the water.

He rowed the little boat away from the ship.

Patrick turned his back to the *Amphion.* He squeezed into the bench next to James and Beth. Beth was breathing hard.

He heard Cookie shout, "Good riddance. You belong in prison, you little thief!"

Henry's face suddenly appeared in a gun port. He shouted and threw another rammer into the water. He waved wildly to them. The three friends waved back.

Patrick turned to Beth. "What happened?" he asked in a low voice. "Why did Cookie call you a thief?"

"I think Onion Jim stole Cookie's gold coin," Beth said. "Then the bird must have hidden it in my pocket. The cook thought I took it."

Patrick nodded. Then he looked ahead of them. A large ship floated in the harbor. It looked the same size as the *Amphion,* but it had no sails. The holes for the gun ports were covered with bars.

The breeze shifted and blew into Patrick's face. He reached up to pinch his nose shut.

"What's that horrible smell?" Beth asked, scrunching up her face.

Patrick never smelled anything that bad in his life. It was even worse than the foul smell down in the hold of the *Amphion*. He wondered if that was what death smelled like.

Their small boat reached a tiny dock that floated next to the ship. A wood plank stretched from the dock to the top deck. Two redcoats stood on the dock. Their muskets glinted in the sun.

One soldier aimed his musket at the prisoners. "Up the plank," he said. "The captain will give you your orders."

Patrick helped Beth climb out of the boat

and onto the dock. They followed James and the other prisoners up the plank. They boarded the ship and looked around.

The deck was crowded with men and boys. Most of them wore torn and dirty clothes.

A British officer stood on an upper deck. He called out for the new prisoners to go line up.

Patrick and Beth and James were marched to the deck below. Rows of dirty hammocks swung back and forth.

James was ordered to report to the cook for food. He left with another group of prisoners. Patrick and Beth were to stay where they were.

Patrick turned to Beth. "We have to help James get away from this horrible place," he said. "If we don't, he'll die."

14

Escape

Below deck Patrick and Beth waited for James. They were with another group of prisoners. Barrels and wooden boxes were on the floor all around them. Hammocks were strung across the walls.

"There you are," James said. He carried a plate of food in his hands. "This is for the three of us."

Beth looked at the leathery slab of meat and frowned.

"The ship's out of fruits and vegetables," James said softly. "All they've got is salt pork. And nobody gets full rations either. Some of the prisoners have been on board more than a year. They're dying from scurvy."

Beth looked at the food on the plate. She wondered how she could eat anything so gray and greasy. The smell made her feel sick.

Beth remembered the onion in her pocket. She took it out.

James's eyes went wide. "Put that away," he whispered. "You'll start a riot."

Beth obeyed. "It's just an onion," she said.

"Onions are a cure for scurvy," James said. "I need to think about how to use it best."

James set the plate on a barrel. Then

he leaned in close to the cousins. "I heard something about a prisoner exchange. The captain's going to swap an American officer for a British officer," he said.

"Lieutenant Prescott?" Beth asked.

James seemed surprised. "Yes," he said. "How do you know him?"

"He helped us," Beth said. She thought for a moment. "Officers are allowed to keep their sea chests, right?"

"Yes," James said. "He'll take his with him."

Beth's face lit up. "That's how you'll escape!" Beth said to James.

"I don't get it," Patrick said.

"James can hide in Lieutenant Prescott's sea chest," Beth said. "They'll carry it off the ship tonight with you inside."

"We'll *all* be inside," James said.

"Wait here," Beth said and ran off.

● ● ●

Later Beth found Lieutenant Prescott near the front of the ship. He was staring at the water.

"May I talk with you, lieutenant?" Beth asked him in a low voice.

The lieutenant nodded and leaned closer to Beth. She whispered her idea to him.

"I leave in half an hour. You'll find my sea chest just outside the captain's cabin," he said softly into her ear. "This is a docked prison ship. The captain doesn't live on board. His rooms are almost always empty. They use the space for storage."

"That's perfect," Beth said.

"But there's a problem," the lieutenant said. "Only one stowaway will fit."

Lieutenant Prescott stood straight and

walked away.

Beth returned to the boys and told them the news.

"You have to go," Beth said to James.

James shook his head. "No," he said. "You're a girl. You go."

"I won't go without Patrick," she said.

"And I won't go with her," Patrick said. "It has to be you. Otherwise, they still might sell you into slavery."

"I can't leave the two of you here," James said.

"We'll be all right," Beth said. "But we have to hurry, or no one will escape!"

They made their way to the captain's cabin. Just outside the door was the sea chest. A boy sat on the floor nearby. He looked sick. His blond hair was falling out in patches. He had sores on his arms.

"Do you have anything to eat?" the boy asked.

James knelt next to him. "How long have you been sick?" he asked.

The boy wearily closed his bloodshot eyes. "I don't know. It's the scurvy, they say." Beth felt sad for the boy. She took the onion out of her pocket. "Maybe you should eat this."

James smiled at her.

Beth peeled the brown skin off the onion. She tore off the roots. Then she handed it to the boy. He bit into it as if it were an apple.

James turned to the cousins and said quietly, "He'll die if he stays here. We must allow him to escape in Lieutenant Prescott's sea chest."

Good-Bye

Beth and Patrick looked at each other. James would lose his chance for escape. But he would save a dying boy. How could they argue with him?

"My name is Daniel Brewton," the boy said. He chomped the last bite of onion. His eyes were teary. Then he wiped his mouth with his hand. He looked up at the three of them and said, "Thank you."

"We have an idea, Daniel Brewton," James

said. He told Daniel what they planned to do.

"You would do that for me?" Daniel asked.

"Of course we would," James said, "You don't want to die on this ship, do you?"

Daniel shook his head slowly. "I've seen others die," he said. "It's horrible."

James opened the sea chest.

Beth lifted out some of the clothes.

Patrick helped Daniel to his feet. "Let's hurry," he said. He thought he heard footsteps come toward them. He helped Daniel lie down inside the sea chest. Beth covered Daniel with the clothes.

James closed the lid. "Shhh," James said to Daniel. "Go to sleep if you can."

Just then Patrick heard a familiar whirring noise. It came from inside the captain's cabin.

"James," Patrick said. "There's a way for us all to escape."

He looked at Beth. She nodded.

James looked puzzled. "How?"

Patrick said carefully, "There's a ship that can take us far away from here. You'll be safe."

"To another country?" James asked.

"Kind of," Beth said.

"You have to trust us," Patrick said.

James thought and then frowned. "I cannot escape if it means taking me away from my duty," he said. "I intend to stay and fight for freedom. Will you promise to take me where I can do that?"

Patrick looked at his cousin. He didn't know what to say. She shook her head. The Imagination Station might take them back to Whit's End. Or it might drop them somewhere else. How could Patrick promise?

James reached out to shake Patrick's hand. "If you can't promise, then I will thank you and say no," he said. "I will stay here to help my countrymen. You should escape if you can."

James shook Beth's hand, too.

Beth gave James a quick hug.

"I have to wonder about this ship of yours," James said. "I suspect you're making it up. But I don't even know where you came from. How did you get on the ship when we first met?"

Patrick heard footsteps again and held up a hand to be quiet.

"We must go," James said. "The guards might search the chest if they see us together."

"We should split up," Patrick said. "You go back to the top deck. We'll go inside the captain's cabin."

James nodded and moved away from

them. He turned just once to look at them. The cousins waved.

James disappeared from sight. Patrick and Beth went into the captain's cabin. They climbed inside the Imagination Station.

"The windshield is fixed," Beth said.

"Good," Patrick said. And he pushed the red button.

Whit's End

Beth and Patrick found themselves back in the workshop at Whit's End. The cousins climbed out of the Imagination Station.

"We made it home!" Beth said.

Beth gave Whit a hug. "What happened?" she asked. "Why didn't the Imagination Station bring us back before?"

Whit rubbed his chin. "That musket ball caused a lot of damage," he said. "It messed up some of the controls. I didn't intend for you to land on that ship."

Patrick and Beth were both surprised.

"When I saw where the Imagination Station took you," Whit said, "I was able to give you the marbles and the onion. But I couldn't do much else until I fixed the controls here."

Patrick said, "But what about James?

I felt terrible leaving him there."

"He gave up his chance to escape," Beth said. "He didn't die on that ship, did he?"

"I'm happy to say he didn't," Whit said. "Better than that, he was released seven months later. He returned home to Philadelphia. He grew up to become a wealthy business owner. He made sails and used his money to fight slavery. He spent his life helping that cause. He wanted *everyone* to be free in America."

Beth asked, "What about Daniel? Do you know what happened to him?"

"Daniel lived. And he never forgot James's kindness," Whit said. "Daniel and James even became friends after the war."

"So everyone had a happy ending," Beth said.

"Not everyone," Patrick said.

Beth and Whit looked at him.

"I went all that way to see the American Revolution. But I didn't get to meet George Washington," Patrick said.

Whit chuckled. "Would you really like to meet George Washington?" he asked.

"Yes!" Patrick said.

"Me, too!" said Beth.

"I think there's just enough time," Whit said.

Patrick looked at Beth. Her eyes were shining. He bolted for the Imagination Station. Beth raced after him. Another adventure was waiting.

To find out more about the next book, *Surprise at Yorktown*, visit TheImaginationStation.com.

Secret Word Puzzle

Unscramble each bold word in the following set of clues. Write the word on the lines provided. Some of the letters have numbers underneath. Write those letters in order on the spaces provided. You'll find the secret word. You'll also know what James Forten gave to the cause of freedom.

ACP

(hint: Beth needed this)

_C_ _a_ _p_
        8

CONNNA

(hint: *KABOOM!*)

_C_ _a_ _n_ _n_ _o_ _n_
3

INOON

(hint: cure for scurvy)

_O_ _n_ _i_ _o_ _n_
             7

Secret Word Puzzle

LAIROS

_s a i l o r_
(1)   (4)

(hint: navy man)

FINEK

_k n i f e_
     (5) (6)

(hint: it's sharp)

SLABERM

_m a r b l e s_
   (2)   (9)

(hint: game)

_s a c r i f i c e_
1   2   3   4   5   6   7   8   9

Questions about this book

Q: Why didn't the British blow up the American's ship?

A: The *Royal Louis* was a valuable prize for the British. The ship, called a man-of-war, was turned into a British ship in 1781.

Q: Did James Forten really turn down an offer to become part of a wealthy family in England?

A: Yes. Captain Bazely offered James the opportunity to be Henry's companion. And James really did turn down the offer because of his loyalty to America.

Q: Did Lieutenant Prescott get into a sword fight on board the *Amphion*?

A: No. Prescott is a make-belive character. But an American officer prisoner did offer James a chance to hide in a trunk.

Join cousins **Patrick and Beth** as they travel back in time to 1781. They arrive just before the final battle of the American Revolution at Yorktown, Virginia. Patrick and Beth sneak through trenches and race across battlefields to warn General George Washington about a dangerous spy. Cannons roar and the ground shakes as the struggle reaches a climax. Washington's ragtag soldiers are up against the most powerful army in the world. Will Patrick and Beth live to witness the American Revolution come to an end? Or will they be caught in a dangerous trap they can't escape?

AUTHOR MARIANNE HERING
is the former editor of *Focus on the Family Clubhouse*® magazine. She has written more than a dozen children's books. She began writing these books for her twin sons, Justin and Kendrick.

ILLUSTRATOR DAVID HOHN
draws and paints covers and pictures for books, posters, and projects of all kinds. He works from his studio in Portland, Oregon.

AUTHOR NANCY I. SANDERS
is the bestselling and award-winning children's author of more than eighty books. She and her husband, Jeff, visited James Forten's house in Philadelphia. Find out more about her at *nancyisanders.com*.